MING'S PICNIC

Written and illustrated by
Stephanie Harris Lang

Burke Publishing Company Limited
*LONDON * TORONTO * NEW YORK*

First published 1987

© Stephanie Harris Lang 1987

CIP data

Lang, Stephanie Harris
    Ming's Picnic — (Head-start story-books)
    I. Title   II. Series
    823'. 914[J] PZ7

ISBN 0 222 01474 1 Hardbound
ISBN 0 222 01475 X Softback

Burke Publishing Company Limited
Pegasus House, 116-120 Golden Lane, London EC1Y 0TL, England.
Burke Publishing (Canada) Limited
Registered Office: 20 Queen Street West, Suite 3000
Box 30, Toronto, Canada M5H 1V5.
Burke Publishing Company Inc.
Registered Office: 333 State Street, PO Box 1740
Bridgeport, Connecticut 06601, U.S.A.

Printed in Great Britain by Purnell Book Production Limited

It was a sunny day.
"Let's go for a picnic," said Mummy.

3

Ming and Mummy made some sandwiches
4 They put them in a basket.

Ming put in crisps,
lemonade and some cups.
Mummy put in a blanket.

Then they set off to the park,
with the baby in the pram.

On the way, they met
Sally and her grandad.

"Would you like

8   to have a picnic with us?" asked Ming.

Oh, yes please,"
said Sally and her grandad.

'We'll buy some food on the way." 9

At the shop they bought two pies,
two bananas, two apples
and four cakes.

In the park
Ming and Sally climbed a tree.

Then they had a hopping race.
Ming won.

Then they had a head-over-heels race.

Sally won.

Then they had a three-legged race.

They both won!

16   "Time to eat our picnic," said Mummy.

Sally's grandad helped
to unpack the food.

18　　　　　　　　　"This is fun," said Ming.

"Food tastes better outdoors,"
said Sally.

After the picnic,
Ming and Sally went to feed the ducks.
The ducks swam across the pond
20 to eat the crusts of bread.

Suddenly — *splash!*
Ming fell into the water.
"Help!" he shouted.

21

Sally pulled him out of the pond
and they ran back to the tree.

Mummy wrapped Ming
in the picnic blanket.

23

"Never mind," said Ming.

24   "The ducks liked their picnic too."